# Street Heat

By Charles Hofer

Illustrated by Dave White

SCHOLASTIC INC.

New York   Toronto   London   Auckland   Sydney
Mexico City   New Delhi   Hong Kong   Buenos Aires

ISBN-13: 978-0-545-02020-6
ISBN-10: 0-545-02020-4

16 15                                                        11 12 13 14/0

Printed in the U.S.A.
First printing, February 2008

It is race day!
Drivers, start your engines.

The first to cross the finish
line will win the race.

It is a long race through the city streets.

The cars go over the
bridge and into the city.

The orange car
takes an early lead!

The streets are narrow here.
It will take a good driver to
win this race.

The black car pulls ahead.
What a move!

There is still a lot of
time left in the race.

This race is tough.
The black car is still in the lead.

Oh, no! The blue car has a flat tire.
The blue car is out of the race.

Here comes the yellow
car on the outside.

The yellow car passes the black car.

The purple car is trying to jump into the lead! What a move!

The drivers must keep
their eyes on the road.

Look out!
The yellow car is driving too
close to the brown car.

They are too close!
The yellow and brown cars
both spin out of control.

Those two cars are out of the race.

Here comes the red car.
The other cars cannot keep up.

# The red car takes the lead.

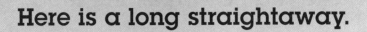
# Here is a long straightaway.

The green car tries to make a
move, but the red car is faster.

The cars go into the tunnel.
They are going fast.

The drivers turn on the
headlights so they can see.

It is the home stretch.

There are three cars out in front.

# This is going to be close!

We have a winner! What a race!